# Tall Tilly

ISBN 0-7696-4051-6

50395

EAN

9 780769 640518

Library of Congress Cataloging-in-Publication Data

Powell, Jillian
    Tall Tilly/ by Jillian Powell; illustrated by Tim Archbold.
        p.cm.—(Lightning readers. Confident reader 3)
Summary: Tilly is not happy with her height until she learns it is an advantage in
sports. Includes vocabulary words and discussion questions.
ISBN 0-7696-4051-6 (pb)
[1. Size—Fiction. 2. Self-acceptance—Fiction.] I. Archbold, Tim, ill. II. Title. III.
Series.

PZ7.P87755Tal 2005
[E]—dc22

                                                            2004060689

Text Copyright © Evans Brothers Ltd. 2004. Illustration Copyright © Tim
Archbold 2004. First published by Evans Brothers Limited, 2A Portman Mansions,
Chiltern Street, London W1U 6NR , United Kingdom. This edition published
under license from Zero to Ten Limited. All rights reserved. Printed in China.
This edition published in 2005 by Gingham Dog Press, an imprint of School
Specialty Publishing, a member of the School Specialty Family.

Send all inquires to:
8720 Orion Place
Columbus, OH 43240-2111

ISBN 0-7696-4051-6

4 5 6 7 8 9 10 EVN 10 09 08 07 06 05

# Tall Tilly

## By Jillian Powell
## Illustrated by Tim Archbold

GINGHAM DOG
PRESS

Columbus, Ohio

Tilly was tall.

She was growing taller every day.

She was taller than all her friends
at school.

In fact, she was the tallest girl in her whole grade.

Tilly could not fit into her clothes.
She was too tall for them.

Tilly could not fit into her bed.
She was too tall for it.

Tilly could not fit into the bathtub.
She was too tall for it.

13

Tilly liked Ben, a boy in her class.
She was too tall for him.

Tilly was too tall to be a ballerina, and that is what she wanted most of all.

Tilly did not like being tall.

She wanted to be short like her
best friend, Molly.

One day, Tilly's teacher had an idea.
She made Tilly the captain of all the
games at recess.

Tilly was good at basketball.

She scored a lot of points for her team.

Tilly was good at soccer.
She stopped a lot of goals from going
into the net.

Tilly was good at running.
She won every race.

Tilly jumped the highest high jumps.

She jumped the longest long jumps.

Tilly was good at every sport.
Everyone cheered for her.

Tilly loved being tall after all!

# Challenge Words

ballerina        goals

cheered        net

# Think About It!

1. Why did Tilly dislike being tall?
2. What did Tilly want most of all?
3. How did Tilly's teacher help her?
4. How many sports did Tilly play?
5. How did Tilly's feelings about being tall change at the end of the story?

# The Story and You

1. Think about Tilly. How would you feel if you were the tallest student in your whole class?
2. Have you ever felt embarrassed about the way you look? Discuss how this made you feel.
3. If you could be the tallest or the shortest student in your class, which would you rather be and why?